Taro Gomi

began his career working as an industrial designer,

and moved into writing and illustrating children's books where he felt

there was more variety and potential for creative expression.

He now has more than 300 children's books, art books

and essay collections in print in Japan. His work has been translated

into more than 10 languages around the world.

Everybody Poos first UK edition 2002 by
Frances Lincoln Children's Books, 74-77 White Lion Street,
London, N1 9PF
www.franceslincoln.com

First UK paperback published in 2004

Originally published in Japan under the title Minna Unchi by
Fukuinkan Shoten, Publishers Inc., Tokyo, 1977
Copyright © Taro Gomi 1977
English text by Amanda Mayer Stinchecum
Copyright © Kane/Miller Book Publishers 1993

British Library Cataloguing in Publication Data
available on request

ISBN 13: 978-1-84507-258-2

Printed in China

19 17 15 13 11 10 12 14 16 18 20

Everybody Poos

Taro Gomi

Translated by Amanda Mayer Stinchecum

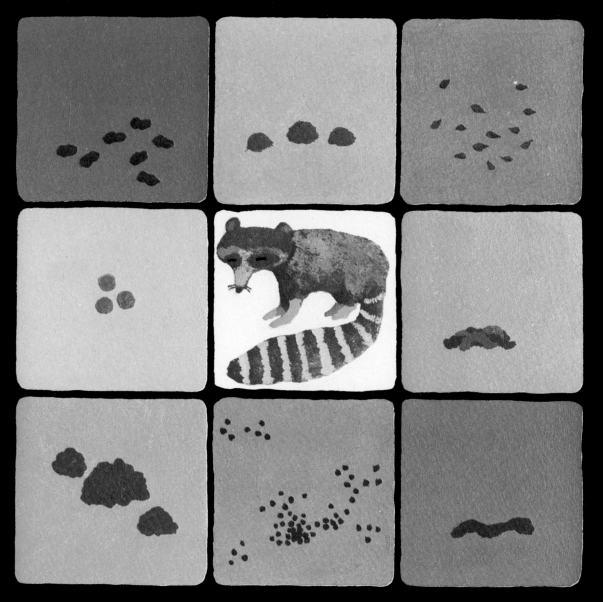

FRANCES LINCOLN

An elephant
makes a
big poo.

A mouse makes
a tiny poo.

A one-hump camel
makes a one-hump poo.

And a two-hump camel
makes a two-hump poo.

Only
joking!

Fish poo.

So do birds.

And bugs
too.

Different
animals
make
different
kinds
of poo.

Different
shapes,
different
colours,
even
different
smells.

Which end is the snake's bottom?

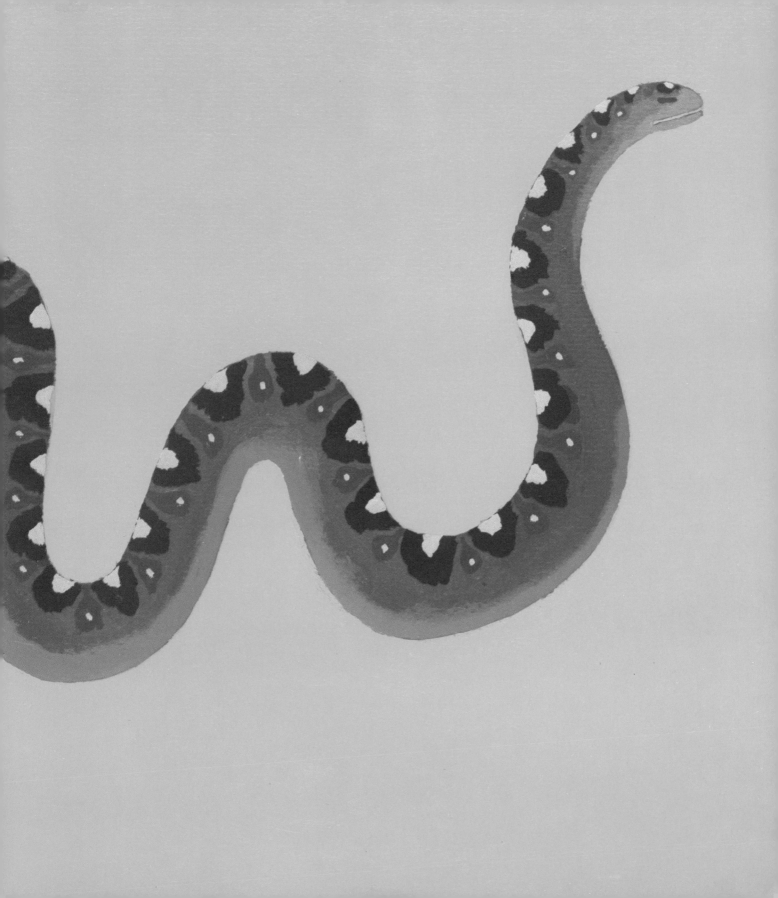

What does whale

poo look like?

Some stop to poo.

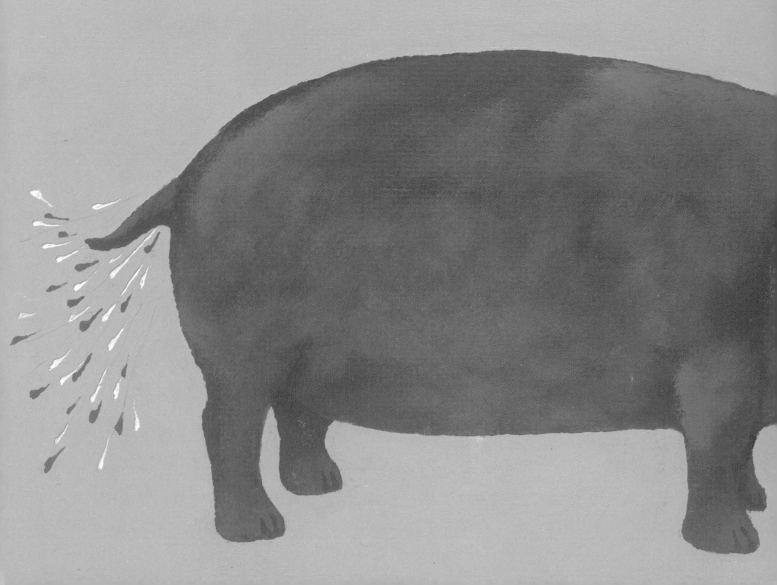

Others do it
on the move.

Some poo here
and there.

Others do it
in a special
place.

Grown-ups poo.

Children poo too.

Some children
poo on
the potty,

others poo
in their
nappies.

Some animals poo and take no notice.

Others clean up
after themselves.

These poo by the water.

This one does it in the water.

He wipes himself with paper

and flushes
it away.

All living things eat, so ...

everybody poos.

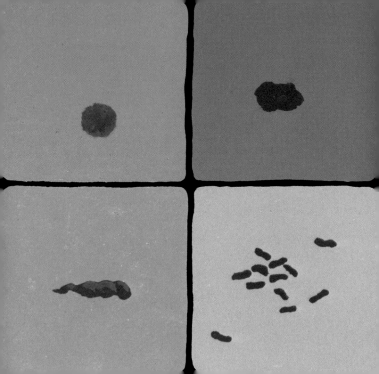

MORE CHILDREN'S BOOKS AVAILABLE FROM FRANCES LINCOLN

The Holes in Your Nose
Genichiro Yagyu

Let's talk about those holes in your nose!
Find out how the holes in your nose help you breathe,
smell and speak, why you sneeze, how bogies are made
and lots of other fascinating things that make the holes
in your nose so important.

All About Me
Debbie MacKinnon and Anthea Sieveking

Stretch, push, jump, explore!
Anthea Sieveking's irresistible photographs capture the vitality
of young children learning about their bodies and themselves.
This very first book is ideal for parents and children to share –
naming, counting, discovering and comparing.

I Have Feelings!
Jana Novotny Hunter
Illustrated by Sue Porter

Everybody has feelings – especially me and you!
Waking up is my best time – then I'm feeling happy. And when we go to the park
I feel really excited. But when my baby sister gets first turn
on the swing, I start feeling jealous!
Small children will fall in love with the adorable star of I Have Feelings! –
an essential book for learning to express your emotions.

Frances Lincoln titles are available from all good bookshops.
You can also buy books and find out more about your favourite titles, authors and illustrators
on our website: www.franceslincoln.com